Candles for Elizabeth

by

Caitlín R. Kiernan

Introduction © 1998 by Poppy Z. Brite
"The Last Child of Lir" ©1997 by Caitlín R. Kiernan. First appeared in *The Urbanite* #8
"A Story for Edward Gorey" © 1997 by Caitlín R. Kiernan. First appeared in *Wetbones* #2
"Postcards from the King of Tides" © 1998 by Caitlín R. Kiernan. First publication.

CANDLES FOR ELIZABETH

An MM Publishing Book
Published by Meisha Merlin Publishing, Inc.
P. O. Box 7
Decatur, GA 30031

Editing & interior layout by Stephen Pagel
Copyediting & proofreading by Teddi Stransky
Cover design by Neil Seltzer
Cover art "Shadowlands" © by Ken Meyer, Jr.

ISBN: 0-9658345-8-1

http://www.angelfire.com/biz/MeishaMerlin

First MM Publishing edition: May 1998

Printed in the United States of America
0 9 8 7 6 5 4 3 2 1

In Memory of Elizabeth Tillman Aldridge

(1971-1995)

"The blood-dimmed tide is loosed, and everywhere
The ceremony of innocence is drowned..."

William Butler Yeats (1920)

Table of Contents

Introduction

It's a gloomy Sunday in February: Mardi Gras parades rained out, needles of water slanting sideways through the air, sky the color of a dead man's eyes. This is the kind of afternoon that Caitlín really likes. No life-affirming horror here, sorry. Sometimes I think Caitlín's characters make mine look like choirboys. But there is more here than will meet the eye of a casual reader looking for escapist thrills.

I once argued with a more traditional horror writer about the works of Kathe Koja. He claimed her characters were affectless and devoid of sympathy: "If they don't give a fuck about anything, why should I give a fuck about them?" A fair enough question, though I don't think the charge applies to all of Koja's characters. More to the point, I'm afraid similar criticism will be levelled at Caitlín's characters, and in her case it is patently unfair. Her characters very definitely give a fuck; it's just that they are terrified to admit it to each other or themselves. They are a motley crew of broken-hearted punks and tough-talking waifs, and some readers will dismiss them with a jerk of the knee as TRENDY, KEWL GOTHS— in the same vein, say, as that awful Poppy Z. Brite. Too bad they'll miss the point of the only horror writer to create a genuine sense of fictional *awe* since Thomas Ligotti, who was the only one to do it since H.P. Lovecraft.

These days it seems as if almost any so-called horror writer you talk to, from the pierced SM vampire-loving freak to the right-wing Christian fundamentalist bomber, will agree that most of the horror fiction being published today is crap. All we have left to argue about is which of us are in the toilet and which of us are the stars (to paraphrase Oscar Wilde as badly as anyone ever has). If we could stop the backbiting for a moment, I think we could all learn something from Caitlín Kiernan. Her work embodies many of the best aspects of *all* horror fiction's myriad traditions.

The three stories in *Candles For Elizabeth* are edgy and bleak; they are also impeccably written and full of a subtle underlying sense of wonder. It would take a hard-hearted reader indeed to see these characters as nothing but a bunch of trendy Goths: they are broken children who would still love to believe in magic and happiness, but don't dare let themselves. They are searching for awe—something any true horror lover should understand.

—Poppy Z. Brite
Feb. 15, 1998, New Orleans, LA

"The Last Child of Lir" originally appeared in Mark McLaughlin's *The Urbanite* (#8, Spring '97). It's one of those stories that occurred to me initially as nothing more than a title, but a title I knew I would eventually find a story for. And the story I found for it was, in part, inspired by a week that I spent in New York City with Christa Faust and Dave Schow in February '96. In particular, a very brisk late night walk through Washington Square: the grand Georgian architecture along the northern edge of the park and the arch itself, ghosts of a lost Manhattan, Henry James' Manhattan, as an almost unnoticed backdrop for the restless scattering of homeless and NYU students, bundled against the cold.

Though it stands on its own, "The Last Child of Lir" is best read (and was intended) as a companion to my stories "Estate" and "Glass Coffin," which can be found in *Dark Terrors 2* (reprinted in *The Year's Best Fantasy and Horror #11*) and *Silver Birch, Blood Moon*, respectively. Anyone unfamiliar with the Irish myth of the children of Lir is referred to Sheila MacGill-Callahan's beautiful adaptation of the story (Dial Books). I owe Leslie Alexander and Christa Faust both a special thanks on this one; *they* know why.

THE LAST CHILD OF LIR

The ass-end of another Manhattan November, fuck Thanksgiving, fuck the goddamn holiday tinsel and Salvation Army Santa Claus bullshit, and Glitch is sitting outside the free clinic, smoking on the steps, No Smoking inside, so here he is in the cold again, fog breath and tobacco cloud from his lips chapped so raw there's blood on the cigarette's filter; waiting for Jamie and Ladybird. Freezing, shivering bundle in his ratty loose army jacket and jeans, watching the concrete gray and brick red of another Village morning. Everyone going somewhere, except him and the black dude across the street, bonethin dude asleep next to a parking meter, bed of plastic milk crates and cardboard, and one blanket the comfortless color of egg custard wrapped tight around him. Maybe he's dead, no way to tell, and Glitch thinks maybe he'll go see, someone should, flicks away the butt of his cigarette and then the door jingles open behind him and this time it's Jamie and Ladybird a few steps behind. Brief scent of antiseptic and warmth from inside before the wind takes it away.

Ladybird, so thin the black guy under the custard blanket looks like the Ghost of Christmas Present and he's clutching an amber prescription bottle in one hand. Jamie huddled in her fake fur cocoon, how many fake leopards had to die for that? staring down at her boots, back turned to the gusts rolling mean down Charlton. "Can I have a smoke?" and so Glitch lights one and hands it to her and finally he asks, "Well?" but nothing volunteered, so "What's the word?" And Ladybird looks up at the sky, bonecheeks and chin like the man in the moon where his pretty face used to be, bags beneath his eyes like bruises. But no answer.

"Yeah, never mind," Glitch says and gets up, starts walking for no other reason than he's sick of sitting outside the clinic watching the dying men and women coming in and going out. May as well be cold somewhere else. They turn up McDougal, heading for the park, the arch, and Jamie's walking as close to him as she can, half a foot shorter and she has to walk twice as fast to keep up. Ladybird somewhere straggling behind. Past a long folding table and someone selling books, piled hardbacks with torn covers that flap in the wind. Ladybird stops to finger through a water-stained copy of *Valley of the Dolls*, ruined and swollen paper, until Glitch tugs at his sleeve, "C'*mon*, man," and they're moving again. Always moving, the time spent between squats and friends' apartments and the hallways outside friends' apartments.

Not so bad at first, late August and the eviction from their TriBeCa ratwarren. August since the band's last gasp, Crimson Stain Mystery buried in yellow pawn slips and the last rung down to the street. Jokes at first, before the cold and Ladybird getting so damn sick, jokes about suffering for their art and the stories they could tell MTV one day. Jamie screaming shit at the suits and ties, the trendy secure, "Punk rock nomads!" and "Kurt Cobain died for your sins!" at the top of her whiskeygravel voice. But whatever gritty romance faded now, like summer and bearable autumn and Ladybird's health. Nothing left but walking and squatting and time like cold, bitter coffee they can't afford.

Before the eviction, Glitch worked making pies and selling slices, him always stinking of tomato sauce and sausage and Jamie always bitching about the smell. And she had a job in a fetish boutique near Broadway, latex and leather, stiletto pumps in men's sizes. Ladybird never working steady, but dancing drag here and there, wherever the pecking order of queens would let him steal a little stage time. So he brought in tips, and once a hundred dollars after he won amateur night at a place without a name, just a neon red tube of lipstick out front. Lipsyncing Concrete Blonde's "Joey," the sort of stuff he always did and the reason why he rarely ever got to perform, no Mariah Carey or Madonna or fucking Whitney Houston. That night, almost perfect night, Glitch and Jamie down front yelling for him so loud they were hoarse for two days.

Never any money from the band, though, just money into the band that should have been going for rent and gas and electricity. Groceries. Toilet paper. A little airtime on a couple of late-nite goth shows, weehour radio for the dead children, one or two mentions in photocopied zines. Jamie's voice and Glitch's oilblack Gibson, Ladybird on bass and a procession of drummers, almost a different one every show until they gave up and paid for a very used drum machine. Worshipping Polly Jean Harvey and Nick Cave so much it showed and they could have been playing covers, the way people stayed away. Might have been different, might have been okay, if they'd sounded too much like Bauhaus or Christian Death, instead.

And then Jamie accused of stealing twenty dollars and lucky they only fired her, lucky they didn't press charges, they said. Glitch never asked if she took the money or not, honestly didn't give a shit. Everyone stole, one way or another; just wishing she hadn't gotten caught, if she had taken the twenty. Always hanging on by their fingernails and without her check bad to worse so fast and one month late on the rent before the old Polish fag super put them out on their butts, their shit out for garbage and the street people to scavenge. Selling what they could, instruments they swore to each other they'd have back before Halloween, Ladybird's dresses and shoes farmed out to other baby queens, the clothes they could carry and a ragged paperback, *The House At Pooh Corner*, into two backpacks and a gym bag. Jamie's boom box and a few tapes. The rest (which really wasn't all that much) just gone.

Glitch trying to keep the pizza job, but that gone too as soon as the owner found out he didn't have an address, "I don't hire bums. You don't even have a place to take a bath. I'll get closed down, kid." And that was that, nothing left but what they could do for each other, and then, finally, what they could do for Ladybird.

Mondays and Thursdays, the three of them hiking or panhandling subway fare to Central Park, the rough stone and castle turrets of the Museum of Natural History, because they know someone who sells tickets, friend of Glitch's from another band years ago and he lets them in, sometimes, if they can manage to look halfway decent. Clean hands and faces, at least, but always *Not my ass if you guys get caught*, always, *I'll swear I never saw you before in my life*, like they've forgotten from the last time. But Glitch nods and thanks him, agreeable, grateful for a few hours' shelter and entry into this one place from the world before, one solid piece to hang onto and keep: church sacred halls and dusty African savannas behind glass, tempera tundra illusions and fiberglass black seafloors. All frozen or suspended, held right there, still point in the chaos and monotony. And the Hall of Dinosaurs best of all, remodeled now and some of its old dignity shined away, solemn shadow traded cheap for sterile interactive flash and Disneyland tricks. But the bones still the same, mostly, holiest reliquary centerpiece and he's been teaching Jamie and Ladybird how to pronounce the names, catechism of Latin and phonetic patience: *Apatosaurus louisae, Oviraptor philoceratops, Tyrannosaurus rex*.

"*You* should'a been a scientist," Ladybird says almost every time, mother voice, no arguing with that tone. "You know *all* this shit," and Glitch shrugs his shoulders, maybe proud inside, and they move on to the next exhibit, mastodons or the mummified duckbill or stuffed Komodo dragons big as jungle cats, mounted fierce and phony gore on their scaly snouts.

Jamie's favorite part a mural, imagined seascape sixty-five million years ago, sandwhite shore and tall cliffs and the sun setting golden warm as honey on the horizon, Maxfield Parrish sky for pterosaur wings, all held inside, within, the tall, cream marble arch; and she says, "I used to dream I could fly," and "That could be a window," as she closes her eyes, smiling soft like she can feel warmer air, clean and tropical twilight breeze, nostrils flared like she's smelling salt.

This isn't Monday or Thursday, just a Tuesday and the three of them sitting together on a bench in Washington Park, huddled close for body heat and company, Ladybird in the middle so he'll stay the warmest; a tape in the box because Ladybird pocketed some batteries yesterday, five-fingered drugstore discount and so Jamie humming along with Patti Smith. Glitch wonders how long before he gets caught, and if he'd be better off if he did, a hospital maybe instead of dying on the street. Even a fucking jail hospital better than dying of pneumonia or toxo or whatever it's going to be, sooner or later, dying out here like a rat or a pigeon or a lousy goddamn wino.

He sees the Bonerman before the Bonerman sees him, standing over near the arch, smoking and talking with some college girls, three girls in identical, impeccable black, and they probably think they're slumming it, cool, talking to a junky. Glitch thinks about getting up, dragging the others after him. Really not in the mood today to listen to Boner's crackhead prattle. But Ladybird's meds have made him sick to his stomach again, ready to puke at the drop of a dime and paler even than usual. So he sits, still and helpless, hoping they won't be noticed, hoping Bonerman will wander away with the NYU chicks or have to hurry off to make his afternoon connection.

"Pretend like you don't see him," whisperhissed at Ladybird, who hasn't and "Who?" so Glitch has to point, one finger jabbed discreet toward the arch and that's enough movement to snag the Bonerman's jittery attention.

"Damn," Glitch mutters, "Never mind."

And Ladybird says, "Oh, *him*" and goes back to looking determinedly nauseous.

"Shit," says Jamie, and by then the Bonerman already past the fountain, cutting across parchment yellow grass to reach them quicker, short, stiff-legged stride, stiff spring in each step, wound so tight maybe he'll explode on the way.

"God, he makes me itch," says Jamie, little mouthcorner sneer and Ladybird says, "Unh-huh," and nods. Glitch pulls his coat tighter, collar up high, turtlehead attempt at retreat. Pointless as spitting into an electric fan and there's the Bonerman and the snotgreen cardigan he's been wearing for weeks, more holes now and raveling yarn, his hair like a malnourished fungus, one brown hand out to pump Glitch's like he can't stop.

Glitch tugs, frees himself, and then the Bonerman starts rubbing his palms together, skin like two frantic sticks, like flint for fire from flesh. "Fuckin' *cold* out here, man," he says, brrrrrrr. "*Too* motherfuckin' cold out here for *my* ass, I sure know that shit."

And, "I heard that," Glitch says.

Jamie's staring off toward Judson Memorial, distant eyes like maybe she's praying he'll go away soon, but Glitch knows she doesn't pray.

"Hey there, Lady," the Bonerman says to Ladybird, winks, and Ladybird sighs, says hey back, most reluctant acknowledgment and anyone else would take it for contempt, but even that much an encouragement to the Bonerman and "You lookin' a little rough today, Lady," he says.

"He's sick," Jamie says, eyes still on the church, "His medicine's making him sick today."

"Oh, man, I'm real sorry to hear that shit," and "Yeah," Ladybird says, "Wanna see me puke?" and his left index finger held up, iceblue polish all but chipped away.

"No, man. But, hey. Look here. I was hopin' I'd run into you guys. I still owe you one, right?" and Glitch has no fucking clue what the Bonerman's talking about but easier to listen than start asking questions.

"You guys still needin' a good squat, right? Sure, and I heard of this place down on West 14th, right down there..."

"We're fine," Ladybird says, interrupting, little gag, dryswallow and then going on, "We ain't so hard up we need to start crashing in crackhouses in the fucking meatpacking district."

Big, offended face from the Bonerman, then, half surprise and half practiced exaggeration, "You don't *look* so fine," pause, and "It ain't like that, it's just this empty warehouse down by the river, okay?" and he's started wringing his hands; that's worse than the rubbing, always drives Glitch bugfuck. And "I was just tryin' to help you guys out, I mean, I'd be down there *myself*, if it wasn't so far away from my peoples and all."

"It's okay, man," Glitch says, sees the storm coming gray and violent behind Ladybird's eyes and so he's talking fast. "Really, thanks, but maybe we should get together about it later. Maybe..." but Ladybird is standing, dizzystagger up from the bench, and the space left between Glitch and Jamie filled in at once with the greedy, eager cold.

"We don't need no favors from fucking *junkies*, okay! We *don't*," and the Bonerman takes a quick step back, two steps, "Hey, bitch! Watch it now," but Ladybird in pursuit, tripping over the boom box, falling and he's vomiting before he hits the sidewalk. The little bit of breakfast they had, stalebland cherry danish split three ways and his third coughed up now on the toes of the Bonerman's duct-taped sneakers.

"*Shit*! Holy Jesus *shit*!" and the Bonerman is staring down at his spattered shoes, the steaming, doughy pink mess all over them and his mouth hanging open stupid, revulsion and surprise fading fast to plain pissed off. "You plague-carryin', Sodomite mother*fucker*..."

And Jamie up before Glitch is even sure what's happened, herself jammed in tight between the Bonerman and Ladybird still dryheaving on the ground. The Bonerman shoves her once, shoves hard and she tumbles over Lady, butt smack right back down on the bench, woodcrack and, "Hey, *hey*," Glitch holding both hands out. "He didn't mean it, Boner. I swear to God and Jesus, man. He didn't mean it. He's just sick, you know? He's just sick."

"Yeah, he's *sick* all right," and "You can catch that shit from puke, man, just like it was blood. Look at my shoes. What the hell am I supposed to do about my shoes?"

And then Glitch is leading the Bonerman away from their bench, apologizing like a broken record, mollifying, desperate silly words and he glances back once to see Jamie kneeling beside Ladybird, arms around him, holding him close.

"Just *look* at my shoes, man," and Glitch does, but nothing he can do, so "I'm sorry as a motherfucker, honest, but it was just an accident." And when he's far enough away that Jamie can't hear and Ladybird can't hear, "Look, about that place, that warehouse..."

"Hey, don't you be askin' me to help your sorry asses out after that shit back there."

And Glitch, "I told you, man. He didn't mean it. The medicine makes him sick. We could really use a safe place. We need to get Lady in out of the cold for just a little while, that's all."

"Yeah, well, I hope the little faggot freezes to death."

"No, you don't," Glitch says, looking back at them again, Jamie helping Ladybird up, lifting him, wiping his mouth with a scrap of something blue from her coat pocket.

"And you owe us, right?" he says, pushing his luck, no luck left so he might as well. The Bonerman is busy cursing and making disgusted noises, smearing his shoes back and forth in the dead grass, stops and stares at Glitch.

"The place is somewhere down by Avenue D," finally, "But I'm just tellin' you so you'll get that fag sonofabitch outta here before I have to cut him or somethin'. I don't owe nobody nothin' after their AIDS-infected fag friend done puked on my fuckin' shoes. That shit makes us even."

One last I'm sorry and Glitch gives the Bonerman fifty cents, quarter and nickel and a bunch of pennies from his pants pockets, miserly compensation but all he has, and then he walks swift back to the bench, leaves the junky alone and still trying to scrape away the stains on his feet.

The warehouse is there, more or less where Glitch had expected from the Bonerman's grudging directions, far enough down 14th he can see dingy steelbluegray glimpses of the Hudson between the buildings. Stinking maze of loading docks and wholesale butchers: diesel fumes, old fat, fresh blood; knives and meat hooks for everything down here. Past concrete and greasy plastic drums marked Inedible - Do Not Eat, and he knows this is the place, derelict, condemned bricks laid a hundred years ago or more and Jamie tells the taxi driver to stop, they'll get out here, please. She pays the fare, precious, crumpled five bucks she's been holding back, gone, the bill and some change, and an ugly look from the driver when she apologizes for having nothing left for a tip.

All afternoon spent talking Ladybird into the move and by then he's running a fever Glitch and Jamie can feel just standing close, cloudy eyes and the soft heat off his skin like he's begun to burn alive in there.

Wet cough and Jamie telling him, finally, that it was going to be the squat or the ER and him giving in, giving up. And now they're all but carrying him, one on each side and his thin arms around their shoulders, not nearly as heavy as he ought to be.

Narrowlong alley squeezed between the warehouse and the building next door and Glitch looking for a way in without leaving obvious tracks, big broken window or busted lock sign for the police or other homeless.

"I don't want to die down here in all this filth," Ladybird says, faint and runny echo of his voice and Jamie frowns, "You're not gonna die, stupid. You just gotta to get out of the wind and get some sleep."

"Oh, and chicken soup, too, please," Ladybird says, "I think I saw a nice, ripe one back there in the gutter." He tries to laugh and winds up coughing instead.

Almost to the end of the alley, dead-end wall and so much colder way back here where the sun never comes.

"Jesus," she says, "Glitch, how are we supposed to get in?" and that makes him flinch, makes him cringe down inside, too tired, ashamed they've come to this, that *she's* come to this: frayed excuse for Jamie like rotten old shoelaces ready to snap, and he sees the hole, then, not big but big enough. Some warped plywood and masonry nails where the bricks have fallen in, but nothing they can't pry open.

"Here," and it feels good to have the answer, any answer would feel good. Lowering Ladybird, careful, to sit against the wall, Glitch's jacket off and spread on the ground for a mat, protection from broken asphalt gravel and the damp. The pocketknife he carries out and he tests the mortar, punkysoft from decades of the river's soggy breath, soft enough to gouge a little furrow without even trying. The knife folded closed again and all his fingers worked into the space between the board and wall, "Help me," to Jamie and both their hands in now, wedged slow, painful between scrubraw brick and splinters, and pulling, more work than he'd anticipated before the nails start to squeal, reluctant, ugly sound, sliding free and her corner pops loose first. *Pop*, and she stumbles, almost falls; one palm sliced, but she's still hanging on.

"You all right?" and she nods, white fog puffs and "Yeah," breathless, "I'm fine, c'mon," and the board comes completely off with the next big tug. From his spot on Glitch's jacket, Ladybird applauds weakly. "My heroes," he mumbles, wide, sloppy smile for them.

And Glitch looks inside, dark so deep and solid he thinks maybe he could scoop up a handful, dark and the musty smell of a place closed away for a very long time.

"Can you see anything?" she says, glancing back down the alley in case their noise has attracted attention and he shakes his head, *no*, and "Well, I don't expect there's much worth seeing," she says.

"Help Lady up," and he ducks inside before he can change his mind, swallowed whole by that black dustreek. Cigarette lighter left in the pocket of his jacket and so he stands up slow, blind and hands out for obstacles. Nothing but the dark, though; his eyes adjusting, gradual, almost imperceptible fade-in from nothing to the dim impression of a large and vacant space, big empty, and neat rows of a lesser darkness on the other side, rectangle smudges one after the other. Windows painted over, and he almost screams when something bumps his legs from behind, rough and sudden nudge, and he reaches back, fingers tangling in hair and it's Jamie, just Jamie.

"*Hey*, will you please watch the fuck out?" she hisses and slaps his hand away.

"There's nothing in here," Glitch says, as they help Lady to his unsteady feet and he's so hot, human furnace and skin slippery; Glitch tries to remember if that's supposed to be a good sign, the sweating, if it means the fever's breaking. Ladybird begins to shiver, teeth chattering like an involuntary reply.

"It isn't the Ritz-Carlton, is it?" Lady wheezes and Jamie says *shhhhhhhh*, but he's already coughing again, awful rattle from his chest that frightens Glitch.

They move slowly away from the hole, bright, hopeless way back, supporting Ladybird between them, three moving as one, bizarre six-legged thing. Something that might belong here, might thrive off this freezing box of night.

"I *can't* die yet," he said, out of his head fevergrin, and "*She* hasn't given me permission...the bitch," that grin and the fear in his eyes glowing hot as his face. But he did, disobedient and dead hardly an hour later, maybe an hour left until dawn. The nest they made for him in one corner of the warehouse, most of their clothes spread out on the icy cement, their coats wrapped around him and Glitch and Jamie shivering through the long night. The batteries running low on the boom box, so the Tom Waits Lady asked to hear playing slower and slower, "Blind Love" and "Walking Spanish" stretched and slurred; Ladybird mummyswaddled and Jamie holding his hand at the end, begging him to let Glitch find a phone, call an ambulance.

"*No*," Ladybird said and squeezed her hand twice as hard, "We made a deal," and they had, a week after the death of Ladybird's last lover and he'd made them both swear it wouldn't be like that for him, no lingering hospitalwhite death scene on antiseptic sheets, plugged into machines to breathe for him and shit for him, while his body wasted down to bone and yellowjaundice skin and things he couldn't even pronounce ate away his brain.

Lady squeezing so hard it hurt, his nails biting her and Jamie pleading. And then he sighed and closed his eyes and wasn't squeezing her hand anymore. And it was over, no debate, no decisions left to make. That simple, that easy.

Neither of them crying, not yet, sitting with his body, without words, their coats retrieved and Jamie brushing his hair, patient fingers working through the day's snarls.

Until, finally, "What do we do with him?" Glitch whispers, and he's glad he can't see her face very well.

No place else to go, and so they stayed there in the old warehouse on 14th Street. Ladybird's body lugged three blocks south the next night and left slumped in a doorway, dead boy alone and no colder than the night around him; Jamie called the police from a pay phone, Glitch telling her it was too dangerous, stupid, and her telling him to fuck off, she didn't give a shit anymore.

Two days later, Jamie sitting in the one small pool of afternoon sun that gets through a high place where the paint has flaked away or the brush missed, sitting alone with *The House At Pooh Corner* and all Ladybird's things stuffed, bulging, into his nylon backpack beside her. Glitch went out for food earlier, came back with a couple of hard bagels and a plastic three-liter Coke bottle full of water. Bread and water, and she just looked at him when he said that, blank eyes, blank face, bread and water, hah fucking hah.

So he goes up to the second floor by himself, wooden stairs past rickety, set way back near an old freight elevator that might still work, if there was electricity. Suicidal dumb climb through the darkness, right hand never leaving the railing and every step like being in the hull of a movie pirate ship, sway and creak, counting the steps for a charm to keep them anchored to the wall: fifteen, eighteen, twenty-one and he's at the top. Heart in his throat, in his fucking mouth, but both feet on the landing, second tier of concrete flooring and it's so dark he only knows that there's a door in front of him because his hand fumbles, blind man lucky, across the knob.

Of course, it'll be locked, he thinks, it absolutely *has* to be locked, right? but the knob turns oilsmooth, faint hasp click as the door swings inward, swings open, and never so much light in the world. Never in this world, never this brilliant and drowning, hands up over his eyes, squinting out between his fingers while his pupils shrink down to make sense of it all; and it's only that they didn't bother to paint out the windows up here. Glitch steps blinking into the looking-glass twin of the room below, sun-choked yang to an ebony yin. Not just the light, though: this room as full as the one downstairs is empty, wall-to-wall stuffed with wooden crates and drop cloths, some of the crates big enough to hold trucks or zoo elephants. The walls resolving to bleached swimming pool blue, rising up to the windows and then a rusty network of steel girders, bare ribs for the pitched roof overhead.

Neat rows, building block neat stacks, and the shoulderwide paths left winding between, shipping crate canyon stretching away from him. Glitch almost turns and calls back down the stairs for Jamie, but stops, goes instead to the nearest line of boxes and touches the one at the bottom, box almost big enough it could hold their last couple of apartments and he touches it. *Checking to see if it's real, really here*, he thinks and aloud, "Bullshit, it's a fucking warehouse ain't it?" His fingers brush cautious across the wood, strong lumber bearing the weight of all the crates piled above for God knows how long. Callused fingertips across the words stenciled there, whatever original red sunfaded now to dullest redorange: DESVERNINE CONSL/LOT 5 and the arrow pointing toward the ceiling or the stars and THIS END UP.

"You have to come see," he says again, as Jamie scoots her butt over a little more, following the drowsy track of the sun, keeping herself in its favor. She looks up at him from the safety of the Hundred-Acre Wood and says, cold as the floor, "I don't *have* to do anything, Glitch."

"It's a whole lot warmer up there. And we'll be safer, okay?" New strategy if she doesn't care about the crates, practical tactic, but she only shrugs and goes back to her book.

"I'm trying to read, Glitch. Just leave me alone."

"Jesus," and he sits down in front of her, arms hugging his own knees, the scuffed toes of his boots almost touching the scuffed toes of hers. He says nothing else for a long time, watches her reading, ignoring him, until the sun's almost down and he knows she can't see the pages anymore.

"You think it was my fault, don't you? Because I brought us down here," and her eyes up again, impenetrable anger for everything they see.

"*I'm* the one that talked him into coming," she says, "Not you. This isn't even about you."

"It was his choice," Glitch says, reaching for her as she pulls away, "Fuck off," and that's all, the book closed, laid aside, and she turns away from him.

He works alone while she sleeps below. Baby aspirin light leaking in from the streets, city light strained through the flyblown windows. A crowbar he found among the crates and the muffled rumble of thunder somewhere far away, storms coming, and he's prying the crates open one after another, carelessly careful not to upset the stacks so it all comes crashing down on top of him. Crying at first, loud and racking sobs that he thinks will never end, will tear him apart, pain enough to eat him alive; but his grief and fury poured into the work, release through tear ducts and straining muscles. And inside each crate a different miracle, Glitch pushing or digging his way through dustdry seas of excelsior and cotton padding to the treasures hidden inside, impossible pearls to find here among the rat nests and spiders.

This shit doesn't even make sense, these things he lifts gently from their prisons with unsteady hands: life's work of a dozen lunatic taxidermists in the first three or four boxes, beautiful horrors, song birds with bat wings, motheaten ape with a crocodile's tail, two-headed bobcat or lynx and the stitches, forgery's fingerprint, plain enough to see through the fur that falls away at his touch. And then a crate filled with a hundred glass jars and each wrapped in moldering straw and brittle newspaper, filled with alcohol or formaldehyde for the scales and spiny fins and skin as pale as cheese floating within. A zoologist's nightmares, too pitiful or perverse for exhibition and Glitch sets down a quart jar of pickled flesh and gristle and smoothes a page of newspaper packing out flat on the lid he's pried away. The *Times* and the date across the top barely legible, February 17, 1943. Thirty years before he was born, ten years before his *mother* was born; half a century or more since these jars were wrapped and secreted away.

Glitch's hand against crumbling newsprint, casual, critical contact of typescript disintegration and his living skin, his twenty-five years and the weighted certainty of time he's never felt anywhere else but the Museum: Hall of Saurischian Dinosaurs, Hall of Ornithischian Dinosaurs and the visible heft of petrified bones. The empty socket gaze of an *Allosaurus* skull and the confined smell from these crates washing over him.

Glitch turns to the next box, picks up the crowbar, crudest tool become a key and another lid comes away, another after that: Roman statues and Egyptian tablets, a skull that he would swear was a unicorn's if he ever believed in unicorns, and all the time he's moving deeper and deeper into the ordered labyrinth of wood and nailsteel, messy trail of uncounted unlikelihoods left behind. Too much left to see, to divulge, for him to pause, give in to lazy curiosity and finally these two crates set apart from all the others. Like they've been waiting here for him all along, at the still heart of this room, heart of this building left for dead.

One tall and narrow, not much larger than a phone booth and the other so long, wide enough to conceal a city bus. *She must be right beneath me now*, he thinks, standing at the center of this room and Jamie asleep in the middle of the one downstairs, Ladybird's things held close to her and FRAGILE redorange across the wood, same as all the ones before, HANDLE WITH CARE. His arms hurt and he tries to remember where he left his coat, barely remembers taking it off, hot and sweatsoaked from exertion despite the cold, despite the wind at the windows.

Go ahead. Open them, and "Oh," he says, "I am so sorry, Lady. I'm so goddamned sorry."

And when he's done and the crates are boards and bent nails, there's no strength left in him to be amazed, the fact of his awe left but not the passion, and so he can only stand and stare and wonder that he still has tears left to cry.

The simple cabinet of glass and fine, varnished wood, that holds the wings, tattered things of ivory and dappled gray, wired stiff on an iron rod and drooping anyway, as many feathers lying scattered at the bottom of the case as left on the wings. Wings that must have once belonged to something huge, a condor he thinks, or an albatross.

And the circus cage, straight off a cardboard carton of Barnum's animal crackers, absurd and ornate frame of wrought iron and bronze filigree, inviolable bars hidden politely behind rotting velvet the gangrenous color of old avocados and when he pushes them aside, ties them back, Glitch can see nothing in there but more straw, more dust. He breaks the padlock with the crowbar, and climbs inside, sits staring back out at the room, the gutted crates, their menagerie of atrocities and treasures scattered about. Outside, it has started to snow, might have been snowing for hours, for all he knows. White gusts hard against the panes and it makes him cold again, seeing the storm, and he wishes he had his coat, though not enough to climb out again and hunt for it. He lies down in the straw and closes his eyes, and in a moment he's asleep.

"I used to dream I could fly," someone says and Glitch turns around to see who, knows her name without her having to tell him, Maeve, tall and her skin like eggshell and chalk on a blazing summer sidewalk. Naked, perfect, and he looks away, back out to the smooth, green sea, the high cliffs where the land drops away, the procession of white-apron men in between, plump and pigsnouted men, marching along with their cleavers and bloodstained feet.

The wind is warm and smells like salt and rain, flows around and through him, lifts him up, above the world and its taut, indifferent soul. His wings are stronger than arms could ever be. His swan voice more beautiful than Jamie's (*Fuck off* she said. *Fuck off* and she walked away with the rabbit and the bear and the donkey's tail in her hand), envy from wheeling gulls and kestrels and jealous pterosaurs. This shimmering freedom beyond the simple absence of restraint and the wild, wild wind draws tears from his black eyes, and they roll off his beak and fall into the sea.

Aware, then, that she's somewhere above him, her shadow and his playing tag over the waves and "*See?*" she asks him, "Isn't it beautiful?" but he's already sipping from the cup his mother has handed him, water or cherry Kool-Aid and the kitchen is filled with their screams, his terrified brother and sisters. Childscreams from birdmouths as bones stretch and snap and bend into new shapes, as feathers burst through their bleeding skin. And Aiofe says, "This one gift I can give you," sarcasm smirk and she lights a cigarette, blows cartoon smoke rings that settle over them, and "They'll hunt you for it, though."

And then Glitch is pulling Jamie back, a handful of sweater and she's leaning so far over the rails, through the arch of milkpale marble into the sunset. Standing on her toes and leaning out, reaching for that last Cretaceous sunset, or Ladybird alone on the beach. His back is turned to them and Maeve says "The others went back to their skins, when they could," but Glitch doesn't care; if there's some lesson in this screw it, he only wants to fly. And, "I couldn't give this up," she cries in notes as sharp as crystal shards and sweet as cream soda.

They ride low now, skimming inches above the whitecaps, dart and shimmer of fishsilver beneath the surface and her banking, leading him back toward shore and the tall, rough cliffs glowing orange as the western ocean swallows the sun and the clouds overhead catch fire.

"He wanted everything terrible for himself," she says, and there's Ladybird, his bare feet in the surf, wickerbrown basket of ammonite shells in his hands. The dead boy smiles and waves as they pass overhead, up past the leathery things that cling to the cliffs, and Jamie's leaning so far out that she'll fall for sure, will tumble head over fucking ass and "He held me for a long, long time. Even after he died, he held me..." and Glitch is pulling Jamie back, both of them falling to the polished museum floor, hitting hard. Glitch bites his tongue, mouthful of coins and needles, but nothing compared with the pain in his shoulder blades as she takes back his beautiful alabaster wings, tears them free and so he holds tight to Jamie, all that's left him; holds her fiercely and will *not* let her go, presses his face into the sticky warmth of her cheek.

And opens his eyes.

"Glitch?" she says, Jamie, standing in the mess of disemboweled crates, holding onto a stuffed and mangy dodo by one stubby leg. "Glitch?" Confused, red eyes, and "What is all this?" He blinks, freezing and stiff all over from the floor of the cage, itching from the straw. Opens his mouth to answer her, and through the bars he sees what's left of the tall display cabinet.

"I had a really bad dream," she says, but Glitch can't take his eyes off the glitter of powdered glass around the cabinet's base, twisted stump of the iron rod that held shriveled gray wings. And nowhere a single fallen feather.

"God, Glitch, I miss Lady so much," and she's crying, crossing the room to him, picking through and over all the shit piled in her way. A big jar kicked over, smashed, and Glitch is crying too, realizes he's been crying since he woke. He feels the draft before he looks up and into the bone and charcoal sky hanging low above the warehouse, and the single broken window, and the snow getting in and falling softly to the floor.

Author's Note: The Irish names Maeve and Aiofe are pronounced May-vuh and *Ay*-fa, respectively.

"A Story for Edward Gorey" was first printed in Paula Guran's magazine, *Wetbones* (#2, Fall '97). I'm endlessly fascinated at the way that artist Edward Gorey manages to seduce his audience into his macabre little stories with images that are so simple as to be almost minimalist, imagery that is very often inexplicable in its malignancy. Why *is* an armless black doll skewered on a piece of wire driven into a ceiling so disturbing? Or what appear to be merely pieces of fabric hanging in the air of a somewhat gloomy room? Or a small boulder resting on a table? A furry, penguin-like creature in tennis shoes? I wanted (and still want) to know if a similar effect can be achieved in prose. "A Story for Edward Gorey" was my first attempt. It was written to Nick Cave and The Bad Seeds' *Let Love In*.

A STORY FOR EDWARD GOREY

The alley so hot and Erica's been watching the dark third-floor window for almost an hour. Dark hole left in the brickwork, dark space so cool and every now and then the lace curtain the color of purple jelly beans moves a little, stirs from the useless summer breeze or maybe someone inside. Maybe a cat stretched out fat and panting on the windowsill, all black cat so Erica can't see it up there, can't even see its slitgreen eyes looking down at her. Erica's neck is starting to hurt, watching the window so long from the alleyshadow. Another half hour and the sun will come up over the rim of the building and she'll have to find another place to stand, or sit, some place out of the noon burn. She lights her last cigarette and sits down so she can lean her head back against something, dumpster steel not hot yet, but not cool either, not like the window.

A month now since she came to Atlanta, too old to be a runaway but the one time she blew a quarter calling home that was what her mother called her anyhow. "Mom, you can't be nineteen *and* a runaway," she said, "I'm legal," and that just made her mother cry. A month and still living on the streets, still begging spare change at Little Five Points, still sleeping wherever; sometimes lucky and someone lets her have a little bit of floor for a night or two, but mostly it's doorways and parks.

And it's still better than home and better than the shitty little white trash planet and her shitty fast food jobs, even now that it's turned summer proper and the nights aren't much cooler than the days. This is *still* better. Even a little sex, a couple of other baby dykes, both younger than her, jailbait girls with their redfresh piercings and sweet, girlsweat smells, so much of what she left home for there between their thighs, beneath their t-shirts.

The curtain moves again and Erica doesn't take her eyes off it, pulls another mouthful from the Camel, smoke out slow through her nostrils but it doesn't move again. Not even really a curtain, just a piece of purple cloth stuck up for a curtain, filter for the sun and the black inside. Probably just nailed up there, or maybe a staple gun instead of nails, but you can't really call that a curtain.

"Shit," she whispers around the cigarette's filter, and the lace is already still again.

Three hours later and the sun up and over, heading back down, fireball pissed off at the whole goddamn world, wanting to set it on fire and coming so close but no cigar. Three hours dodging a couple of cops and hanging around outside the stores, catching the tourists and the hipster kids spending Daddy's money on their way out or in. Better when they're on the way out, holding plastic or paper bags of clothes or shoes or CDs, red-handed, easy marks. Guilt to grease the gears— she's getting good at this, tips from Vincent and a couple of others who've been here a lot longer than she has. More than five dollars this afternoon, most of it quarters and the pockets of her baggy gray trousers feel ready to burst, duct tape on the seams but they jingle a little when she walks and bump hard against her legs. She rests a few minutes in the tiny plaza across from the shop that sells crystals and wind chimes and tarot cards, brown grass and crape myrtle trees, watches the board weasels kicking around their hackey-sack ball and the Rasta woman trying to sell her beads and incense sticks.

"Hey bitch," and when she turns around it's just Bennie, little Bennie in her too-big overalls and the same L7 t-shirt worn a week now, starting to look like someone washed a car with it or something. Head shaved closer than Erica's, down to skin and just a little yellow fuzz. "Hey, Bennie," Erica says and Bennie sits down beside her. "Got a cig?" and Bennie shakes her head no, and "Fuck. That figures."

"There's a party tonight," Bennie says and scootches closer, close enough that Erica can smell her, b.o. and the vanilla oil she wears. "I don't know the people but it's supposed to be free and we could go, if you want. There'll be beer, at least, and a dj. We could dance…"

"Sure," doesn't know if she means it, the way Bennie almost always winds up getting on her nerves, but "Sure," anyway and so a big smile from Bennie.

"Cool. Hey, look, I gotta go find someone, but let's meet back here later, okay?" Erica nods, and Bennie hugs her, quick cheek kiss, and then she's gone and the hot air still smells like her. Erica stares up at the sun through the crooked little branches and thinks about the alley and the lace curtain. Late enough there's probably shade again by now, if she can stand the stink from the dumpster. Worth the sour curry rot from the Indian restaurant's garbage, worth a little funk to watch that cool black hole.

The smell even worse than she expected, all the fresh and not-so-fresh crap in the dumpster baked by the July sun and she bets if she peeked inside there'd be maggots. She sits down a few feet from the dumpster and wishes she'd remembered to stop at the Jiffy Mart for smokes on her way, sucks on a pinkie finger instead. Watches, the red and chocolate bricks, dull red-orange like lipstick and chocolate brown like semi-sweet Hershey bars, old bricks worn as wrinklesmooth as the skin of old women. And the black window and the purple lace. No air conditioning or the window wouldn't be open, probably, but she can imagine, knows how cool the air past that curtain must be. No heat to that quality of dark, blessed sanctuary chill of supermarkets, frozen food aisles, heavy air, and *maybe* if she stood directly under the window some might come pouring out and down the wall, spill right over her.

And the face at the window, then, so white and sudden she jumps, startled, caught, tries to look like she wasn't sitting there staring in, peeping tom, nosy pervert. But those eyes squinting down at her, nowhere to go unless she fucking runs, and the woman says "Who are you?" Voice as cool as ice cream sandwiches, Georgia drawl that doesn't seem to match such perfect, porcelain skin.

Erica doesn't answer, tongue gone to lead, dead meat in her mouth; she just stares back, deaf-mute idiot stare until the woman shakes her head, hair so black it's hard to see, frame for that face, white hands braced on the windowsill, nails long and polished but Erica can't tell what color.

"What? Do you think people never look out their windows?"

And Erica's talking, tongue unlocked and moving before she can hold it back. "I really like your curtains," she says, stupid, goddamn stupid thing to say, but the woman smiles at her, surprised eyebrows, and "My curtains? *This*?" and tugs at the purple lace. "You like *this*?"

"Um, yeah. I do," and before she can say anything else the woman asks, "What's your name?" so at least she can say something that makes sense. "Erica," she says. "My name's Erica," and the beautiful, pale woman in the cool, black window says "You wanna come up for a while, Erica?"

"Uhm," and Erica glances back toward the street, the asphalt melt and concrete glare, and the pale woman says, "I could fix you a glass of iced tea. If you wanna come up, I'll buzz you in. You like iced tea with mint?" and all Erica can think about is how the woman's skin would feel, white and so smooth, marble statue chill; to be held in arms like that, arms to take away the fever for a little while. "Erica?" the woman says, and Erica nods, "Yeah. Yeah, sure."

Big freight elevator with silver walls to shine back dull; scratched and dull Erica looking back at herself in smeary reflections and above her head the constant hiss and electric fluorescent buzz. The elevator smells like old piss and makes an ugly, pinging noise as it counts off the floors, two, three and the blurry Erica watching her splits down the middle, pulled apart as the doors slide reluctantly open. She steps out, anxious to be free of that clanking mirror box, steps out into the long hall and the only light up here coming in through a window way down at the other end, but bright enough that she can see the plaster walls painted dark red or maroon, worn carpeting to match. And the air stifling, soupy thick, no better than the street, maybe worse for the odors getting out past the unnumbered doors she passes, each one a different color like big, dingy Easter eggs.

The blue door, the woman in the window said, but here's a door the bleached blue of empty swimming pools and the next one down gaudy bright like peacock feathers. Erica knocks on the swimming pool door, hesitant knock, uncertain knuckles on wood, and Jesus, she's sweating, nerves and the heat and maybe this was a bad idea, maybe she shouldn't be bothering people she doesn't know. But the unlocking sounds begin before she can change her mind, safety chain rattle and hard deadbolt click; "Hi, Erica," the woman says when the door swings open, "Come inside."

Immediate disappointment, the apartment dark but almost as hot as the hall, stuffy and nothing but a noisy little electric fan, antique store relic on the floor recycling the sticky air. She tries not to *look* disappointed, smiles and shakes the woman's hand, which isn't cool either. Sweatslick palm and Erica says, "It was awful nice of you to ask me up."

An hour later and Erica lying naked and exhausted on the woman's bed, black sheets, ebony wrought iron and the filmy white canopy like spider silk. A slight breeze slips in through the open window, late afternoon smells, light breeze to finger the lace curtain and *I'm on this side*, she thinks. And it's such a strange and simple thought: *I'm on this side*.

The woman has gone to the kitchen again, gone for more of the sweet, minty tea, the woman named Isabel, and so Erica lies very still, listens to the music coming from the expensive stereo (when asked, *I mostly like rap*, she said, and the woman smiled and put on classical) and stares at the apartment around her. Mostly just this one big room filled up with furniture, as far as she can tell; stuff like she remembers from the old lady houses her mother used to clean back home. Burgundy velvet sofa and high-backed chairs of dark, carved wood, something that isn't a chair or a sofa, something in between, but Erica doesn't know what it's called. Brass lamps with softly glowing stained glass shades like wisteria and dragonflies, satin shades with beaded fringe; a huge oriental rug covering most of the floor, hardwood crust around the tattered edges, crimson and gold weave worn thin by feet and dust and time. Walls lined with tall, lighted display cabinets and a patchwork of pictures in expensive-looking frames, pictures hung almost all the way up to the tall ceiling, hardly an inch of bare wall left anywhere.

The pictures are pretty, landscapes and women too beautiful to ever be real, but the cabinets are crowded with old books and bones, rocks and stoppered jars. Jars filled with murky liquid and dead things floating inside, and she doesn't like to look at them. Doesn't like to think about the staring milky eyes, or what might be in those books, so she just looks at the pictures instead.

And then the black doll, unnoticed all this time, dangling from the ceiling near the open window. What might be a coat hanger bent open and one end run straight through its cloth body, the other end twisted closed around a small hook set into the plaster. Featureless thing, raglimp legs hanging down and no arms at all; only smooth, blank nothing where a face might be.

"Do you like Maxfield Parrish?" the woman asks, and Erica makes herself look away from the awful doll. Isabel carrying a silver serving tray and two tall glasses, tea and ice cubes and a green sprig of fresh mint on each. She sets the tray on a table beside the bed, offers one glass to Erica. It's slippery with condensation, so cold it almost hurts to hold.

"Is that who painted all these pictures?" and the woman sits down beside her, sips from her own glass.

"Not all of them, but most," she says.

The sudden screech of tires outside, car horns, and Isabel rubs her glass across her forehead.

"That one, up there," and Erica follows her finger, grateful she's not pointing in the direction of the black doll. "That's 'Salammbô.' It was painted by Gabriel Ferrier in 1881."

The painting high on the wall, a woman with skin as pale as snow, paler than Isabel's, lying on a bed and an enormous snake, python or boa constrictor, twined tight around her body. In the background, another figure, indistinct man or woman playing what looks like a harp. The snake poised to strike or kiss and the woman, lips parted slightly, eyes half-mast, impossible to tell if that's pleasure or pain, if she's fainted, and Isabel's already pointing to another, even further up the wall, almost lost in shadow. Erica has to strain to see.

"That one's by Antoine Magaud. I don't remember the year," and it's another woman, standing before an elaborately framed mirror, dress down and maybe a hint of her breasts, lips pressed gently to the looking glass, to the reflection of her lips.

"It's called 'A Kiss in the Glass.'"

"Are they real?" and Isabel laughs, but not a mean laugh. "No, dear. They're only prints."

"Oh," and she feels so sleepy, so long since she's been this comfortable, anything like this content and Isabel is taking the glass from her hand. "Take a nap," she says, "I hate to think where you've been sleeping," and Erica's already closing her eyes, uneasy glance back to the black doll to see it still there, thinks maybe she can see a place where a stitch has raveled and a bit of stuffing is poking out, cotton as black as the cloth. But she can't see it with her eyes shut, and Isabel's fingers, her long nails the color of evergreens, feel so good against Erica's scalp. Softest kiss at her ear, warmth and a whispered confidence, something Erica knows she won't remember, before she's asleep.

This old house down near the creek, through the woods behind her mother's house. Old house where a black man used to live, but doesn't anymore. Nothing left of him now, bare floor, bare walls, ghosts of pictures marked by less faded wallpaper patches. Wallpaper peeling like skin in calico strips and molding house bones underneath. Erica's sitting in a corner, hard wooden chair that hurts her butt, straight back and the sun so bright outside. Bright as the butterfly sparrows lighting on the eaves of busted windows, staring in, waiting.

"Hide them," the girl says, the girl that was the woman named Isabel only a moment ago but now she's a girl, Tonya making wads from magazines at the fireplace. Pages torn and crumpled, tossed in with twigs and pine straw tinder. "Jesus, Erica, you said nobody would know. You said nobody would ever find out."

And Tonya's striking a match, big kitchen match, wood and little redwhite sulfur head to blaze. *Scritch*, and all the magazines are burning. All the pretty women eaten by the flames, swallowed by the crackle and rising up the chimney, bare breasts and hips and lips and eyes to rising flakes of shitbrown ash. The room smells like the sun and burning paper.

"I'm sorry," she says and "There's no point in being *sorry*, Erica," Tonya says. "Sorry's not gonna make it better. My daddy's gonna beat the shit outta me."

And the clopping sound as the little horses march across the floor, the pretty plastic horses, palominos and stallions black as midnight, ponies the color of pecans, marching to the fire. Tonya doesn't do anything to stop them; crying now and they gallop past her, more fuel for the hungry fire.

"You don't care what people think of you," Tonya sobs and smears snot and mascara with the back of her hand. "You're just a fucking dyke, anyway."

Something Erica wants to say, comfort or self-defense, but the clopping grown so loud now, so many little horses and when she says "No, Tonya," she can't even hear herself.

"I just don't know what to do, I just don't," and why can she hear Tonya? Why can't she get up and step over the fucking horses and shake Tonya and make her stop? "I just don't know," Tonya's words like the straight razor in her hand and the greenblue veins in her wrists. And Erica sees it on the mantle, then, the black doll, slumped over so the empty place where its face should be is hidden.

clop clop

"He'll send me off somewhere…" and the black doll is falling forward, tumbling (*clop clop*) into the brilliant space between the beat of tiny horseshoes, between Erica and Tonya, the sun white light flashing off the razor's blade and it's a long way down to the floor.

"I *asked* you who the hell she *is*?" the man's voice says again, growls like a dog on a chain, and Erica's lying very still beneath the

sheets, head still too full of the dream to think. Big man voice somewhere in the darkened room and she can still hear the horses, their hooves
against the floorboards of the old shack so maybe she's *still* dreaming.

"She's none of your goddamn business, Eddie," and Erica
knows the clopping noise is coming from the same place as the
woman's voice, off towards the kitchenette and she opens her eyes
halfway. Flickering light like candles and it must be very late, after
dark and she'll have missed Bennie, missed the party. The clopping
stops and starts again.

No, not clopping. Chopping. She's cutting something up in there
and Erica's too afraid to move.

"If you're fuckin' the little bitch in *my* bed, it is too my goddamn
business," the man says and something breaks, muffled shower of glass
across the rug and Erica flinches but doesn't close her eyes again. Moves
her head so slow until she can see the kitchen counter, Isabel's face in
the glow of a white pillar candle.

"It's not *your* bed, Eddie. You don't own the bed or me, okay?
You don't own shit."

And she brings the knife down again, steel into cutting board
wood, the broad butcher's blade glinting and Erica risks another inch,
her face slow across the pillow.

"You're a fucking whore, Isabel," the man says, and Erica imag-
ines the maddog foam on his lips, spit flying from clenched teeth, sharp
maddog teeth. "A goddamn fucking whore. How old is *this* one, anyway? Huh? How old is she?"

The blade down and into something soft she can hardly see from
the bed, meaty lumps and shreds, deepest, stringy red, wet smears on the
blade as it rises again and now a bit of something stuck to the metal.

"How much are we gonna have to pay this one to keep you out
of jail, Isabel?"

Isabel moves, turns quick to face the place the dog man's voice
is coming from and Erica can see her, her hair wild around her white
face, wild tangle and eyes like the sky before a summer storm. And her
lips sticky red, sticky smear across her chin and throat.

"Get the fuck *away* from me, Eddie! *Now!*" and she's pointing
the knife, arm outstretched and that blade at the end, rigid muscles trem-
bling and more smears on her hand and arm all the way up to the elbow.
"I'll cut your fucking throat if you don't leave me the hell alone!"

"Yeah, well, fuck you," he says. "Okay? *Fuck you*, Isabel. I'm not going to be here this time, all right? So fuck you. I don't care if you screw every little dyke in the whole city."

When the door slams, it sounds like a shotgun and all the pictures rattle on the walls, nervous, brittle rattle from inside the display cases and Erica closes her eyes again. Doesn't want to see any more, those eyes and the raw, red stains on those lips. In the dark behind her eyelids, there's only Isabel crying, loud sobs and maybe words stuck in between. And finally, bare feet across the floor, another door opening and closing before the desolate, choking sound of vomiting.

And later, an hour or longer, when there's nothing to hear but the street noise getting in through the open window and the muted voices from other apartments, Erica gets up, gathers her raggedy clothes and dresses quickly, moving catslow and as quiet as she's able but every sound magnified times ten anyway—bed springs and her feet, the jingle of all those quarters and nickels and dimes in the pockets of her pants.

Past the bed, and she's careful not to look into the kitchen, extra careful not to see whatever's left on the cutting board and countertop. But she does turn, not wanting to turn, and the black doll is still there, strung on its wire. The tear in its side seems wider than before, a little more of its dark stuffing showing, and that's probably only a trick of the candlelight; she turns her back on the black doll and "I'm sorry, Isabel," whispered to the closed bathroom. When there's no answer, Erica opens the front door and pulls it silently shut behind her.

Outside, the hall is dark and very, very hot.

Tam and the androgyne twins of "Postcards from the King of Tides" first appeared in my short story "Bela's Plot" (published in Poppy Z. Brite's *Love In Vein II*, January '97). As I often do when I'm writing short fiction, I discovered afterwards that I wanted to spend a lot more time with the central characters. Christa Faust (she does keep turning up, doesn't she?) and I were returning to Los Angeles from Eugene, Oregon and the 1996 World Horror Convention, gawking like tourists at redwoods and Pacific vistas, reading Katherine Dunn's *Geek Love* aloud to one another, when the first inklings of this story came to me. A few hours later, right after dark, we became hopelessly lost in the Klamath Mountains (a name that seems straight out of Lovecraft) east of Eureka and spent the entire night winding along a dirt road so narrow there was no way to even turn around. The title was suggested by George Darley's poem, "The Rebellion of the Waters" (1822), and the story was written primarily to The Sisters of Mercy's *First And Last And Always* and Nine Inch Nails' *The Downward Spiral*. Special thanks to John Pelan on this one.

POSTCARDS FROM THE KING OF TIDES

Here's the scene: The three dark children, three souls past twenty but still adrift in the jaggedsmooth limbo of childhoods extended by chance and choice and circumstance, their clothes impeccable rags of night sewn with thread the color of ravens and anthracite; two of them fair, a boy and a girl and the stain of protracted innocence strongest on them; the third a mean scrap of girlflesh with a blacklipped smile and a heart to make holes in the resolve of the most jaded nihilist but still as much a child as her companions. And she sits behind the wheel of the old car, her sagegray eyes straight ahead of her, matching their laughter with seething determination and annoyance, and there's brightdark music, and the forest flowing around them, older times ten hundred than anything else alive.

The winding, long drive back from Seattle, almost two days now, and Highway 101 has become this narrow asphalt snake curving and recurving through the redwood wilderness and they're still not even as far as San Francisco. Probably won't see the city before dark, Tam thinks, headachy behind the wheel and her black sunglasses because she doesn't trust either of the twins to drive. Neither Lark nor Crispin have their licenses, and it's not even her car; Magwitch's piece-of-shit Chevrolet Impala, antique '70s junk heap that might have been the murky green of cold pea soup a long, long time ago. Now it's mostly rust and bondo and one off-white door on the driver's side. A thousand bumper stickers to hold it all together.

"Oooh," Lark whispers, awevoiced, as she cranes her neck to see through the trees rushing past, the craggy coast visible in brief glimpses between their trunks and branches. Her head stuck out the window, the wind whipping at her fine, silkwhite hair and Tam thinks how she looks like a dog, a stupid, slobbering dog, just before Crispin says, "You look like a *dog*." He tries hard to sound disgusted with that last word, but Tam suspects he's just as giddy, just as enchanted by the Pacific rain forest, as his sister (if they truly *are* brother and sister; Tam doesn't know, not for sure, doesn't know that anyone else does either, for that matter).

Caitlín R. Kiernan

"You'll get bugs in your teeth," he says. "Bugs are gonna fly right straight down your throat and lay their eggs in your stomach."

Lark's response is nothing more or less than another chorus of "ooohs" and "ahhhs" as they round a tight bend, rush through a break in the treeline and the world ends there, drops suddenly away to the mercy of a silveryellowgrey sea that seems to go on forever, blending at some far-off and indefinite point with the almost color-less sky. There's a sunbright smudge up there, but sinking slowly westward, and Tam looks at the clock on the dash again. It's always twenty minutes fast, but still, it'll be dark a long time before they reach San Francisco.

Tam punches the cigarette lighter with one carefully-mani-cured index finger, nail the color of an oil slick, and turns up the music already blaring from the Impala's tape deck. Lark takes that as her cue to start singing, howling along to "Black Planet," and the mostly bald tires squeal just a little as Tam takes the curve ten miles an hour above the speed limit. A moment in the cloudfiltered sun, blinding after the gloom, before the tree shadows swallow the car whole again. The cigarette lighter pops out, and Tam steals a glance at herself in the rearview mirror as she lights a Marlboro: yesterday's eyeliner and she's chewed off most of her lipstick, a black smudge on her right cheek. Her eyes a little bleary, a little red with swollen cap-illaries, but the ephedrine tablets she took two hours ago, two crim-son tablets from a bottle she bought at a truck stop back in Oregon, are still doing their job and she's wider than awake.

"Will you sit the fuck down, Lark, before you make me have a goddamn wreck and kill us all? Please?" she says, smoky words from her faded lips and Lark stops singing, pulls her head back inside and Crispin sticks his tongue out at her, fleshpink flick of I-told-you-so re-proach. Lark puts her pointy, black boots on the dash, presses herself into the duct-taped upholstery, and doesn't say a word.

They spent the night before in Eugene and then headed west, followed the meandering river valleys all the way down to the sea before turning south toward home. Almost a week now since the three of them left Los Angeles, just Tam and the twins because Maggie couldn't get off work, but he'd told them to go anyway; she didn't really want to go without him, knew that Lark and Crispin would drive her nuts without

44

Magwitch around, but the tour wasn't coming through L.A. or even San Francisco. So she went without too much persuading, *they* went, and it worked out better than she'd expected, really, at least until today.

At least until Golden Beach, only thirty or forty miles north of the California state line and Crispin spotted the swan neck of a *Brachiosaurus* towering above shaggy hemlock branches and he immediately started begging her to stop, even promised that he wouldn't ask her to play the P.J. Harvey tape anymore if she'd Please Just Stop and let him see. So they lost an hour at The Prehistoric Gardens, actually paid money to get in and then spent a whole fucking hour wandering around seventy acres of drippywet trees, listening to Crispin prattle on about the life-sized sculptures of dinosaurs and things like dinosaurs, tourist-trap monstrosities built sometime in the 1950s, skeletons of steel and wood hidden somewhere beneath sleek skins of wire mesh and cement.

"They don't even look real," Tam said, as Crispin vamped in front of a scowling stegosaur while Lark rummaged around in her purse for her tiny Instamatic camera.

"Well, they look real enough to *me*," he replied and Lark just shrugged, a suspiciously complicit and not-at-all-helpful sort of shrug. Tam frowned a little harder, no bottom to a frown like hers, and "You are really such a fucking geek, Crispy," she said under her breath but plenty loud enough the twins could hear.

"Don't call him that," Lark snapped, defensive sister voice, and then she found her camera somewhere in the vast, blackbeaded bag and aimed it at the pretty boy and the unhappy-looking stegosaur. But, "A geeky name for a geeky boy," Tam sneered, as Lark took his picture; Crispin winked at her, then, and he was off again, running fast to see the *Pteranodon* or the *Ankylosaurus*. Tam looked down at her wristwatch and up at the sky and, finding no solace in either, she followed zombie Hansel and zombie Gretel away through the trees.

After The Prehistoric Gardens, it was Lark's turn, of course, her infallible logic that it wasn't fair to stop for Crispin and then not stop for her and, anyway, all she wanted was to have her picture taken beside one of the giant redwoods. Hardly even inside the national park and she already had that shitty little camera out again, sneaky rectangle of woodgrain plastic and Hello Kitty stickers.

And because it was easier to just pull the fuck over than listen to her snivel and pout all the way to San Francisco, the car bounced off the highway into a small turn-around, rolled over a shallow ditch and across crunchsnapping twigs; Lark's door was open before Tam even shifted the Impala into park and Crispin piled out of the back seat after her. And then, insult to inconvenience, they made Tam take the photograph: the pair of them, arm in arm and wickedsmug grins on their matching faces, a mat of dry, cinnamon needles beneath their boots and the boles of the great sequoias rising up behind them, primeval frame of ferns and underbrush snarl all around.

Tam sighed loud and breathed in a mouthful of air so clean it hurt her Angeleno lungs and she wished she had a cigarette, then *Just get it the fuck over with*, she thought, sternpatient thought for herself. But she made sure to aim the camera just low enough to cut the tops off both their heads in the photo.

Halfway back to the car, a small squeal of surprise and delight from Lark and "*What?*" Crispin asked, "What is it?" Lark stooped and picked up something from the rough bed of redwood needles.

"Just get in the goddamned car, okay?" Tam begged, but Lark wasn't listening, held her discovery out for Crispin to see, presented for his approval. He made a face that was equal parts disgust and alarm and took a step away from Lark and the pale yellow thing in her hands.

"*Yuck*," he said, "Put it back down, Lark, before it bites you or stings you or something."

"Oh, it's only a banana slug, you big sissy," she said and frowned like she was trying to impersonate Tam. "See? It can't *hurt* you," and she stuck it right under Crispin's nose.

"*Gagh*," he moaned, "It's *huge*," and he headed for the car, climbed into the back seat and hid in the shadows.

"It's only a banana slug," Lark said again. "I'm gonna keep him for a pet and name him Chiquita."

"You're going to put down the worm and get back in the fucking car," Tam said, standing at the back fender and rattling Magwitch's key ring in one hand like a particularly noisy pair of dice. "Either that, Lark, or I'm going to leave your skinny ass standing out here with the bears."

"And the sasquatches!" Crispin shouted from inside the car and Tam silenced him with a glare through the rear windshield.

"Jesus, Tam, it's not gonna *hurt* anything. Really. I'll put it in my purse, okay? It's not gonna hurt anything if it's inside my purse, right?" But Tam narrowed her mascara smudgy eyes and jabbed a finger at the ground, at the needlelittered space between herself and Lark.

"You're going to put the motherfucking worm *down*, on the ground," she growled, "and then you're going to get back in the motherfucking car."

Lark didn't move, stared stubbornly down at the fat slug as it crawled cautiously over her right palm, leaving a wide trail of sparkling slime on her skin. "No," she said.

"*Now*, Lark."

"No," she repeated, glanced up at Tam through the cascade of her white bangs. "It won't hurt anything."

Just two short, quick steps and Tam was on top of her, almost a head taller anyway and her teeth bared like all the grizzly bears and sasquatches in the world. "Stop!" Lark screeched. "Crispin, make her stop!" She tried too late to turn and run away, but Tam already had what she wanted, had already snatched it squirming from Lark's sticky hands and Chiquita the banana slug went sailing off into the trees. It landed somewhere among the ferns and mossrotting logs with a very small but audible *thump*.

"Now," Tam said, smiling and wiping slug slime off her hand onto the front of Lark's black Switchblade Symphony t-shirt. "Get in the car. *Pretty* please."

And for a moment, time it took Tam to get behind the wheel and rev the engine a couple of times, Lark stood, staring silent toward the spot in the woods where the slug had come down. She might have cried, if she hadn't known that Tam really would leave her stranded there. The third rev brought a big puff of charcoalsoot exhaust from the Impala's noisy muffler and Lark was already opening the passenger-side door, already slipping in beside Tam.

She was quiet for a while, staring out at the forest and the stingy glimpses of rocky coastline, still close enough to tears that Tam could see the wet shimmer in the windowtrapped reflection of her blue eyes.

So the highway carries them south, between the ocean and the weathered western slopes of the Klamath Mountains, over rocks from the time of Crispin's dinosaurs, rocks laid down in warm and serpent-haunted seas; out of the protected cathedral stands of virgin redwood into hills and gorges where the sequoias are forced to rub branches with less privileged trees, mere Douglas fir and hemlock and oak. And gradually their view of the narrowdark beaches becomes more frequent, the toweringsharp headlands setting them one from another like sedimentary parentheses.

Tam driving fast, fast as she dares, not so much worried about cops and speeding tickets as losing control in one of the hairpin curves and plunging ass-over-tits into the fucking scenery, taking a dive off one of the narrow bridges and it's two hundred feet straight down. She chain smokes and has started playing harder music, digging through the shoebox full of pirated cassettes for Nine Inch Nails and Front 242, Type-O Negative and Nitzer Ebb, all the stuff that Lark and Crispin would probably be whining like drowning kittens about if they didn't know how pissed off she was already. And then the car starts making a sound like someone's tossed a bucket of nails beneath the hood and the temp light flashes on, screw you Tam, here's some more shit to fuck up your wonderful fucking afternoon by the fucking sea.

"It's not supposed to do that, is it?" Crispin asks, back seat coy, and she really wants to turn around, stick a finger through one of his eyes until she hits brain.

"*No*, Einstein," she says instead, "It's not supposed to do that. Now shut up," settling for such a weak little jab instead of fresh frontal lobe beneath her nails. The motor spits up a final, grinding cough and dies, leaves her coasting, drifting into the breakdown lane. Pavement traded for rough and pinging gravel and Tam lets the right fender scrape along the guardrail almost twenty feet before she stomps the brakes, the smallest possible fraction of her rage expressed in the squeal of metal against metal; when the Impala has finally stopped moving, she puts on the emergency brake and shifts into park, turns on the hazard lights.

"We can't just stop *here*," Lark says, and she sounds scared, almost, staring out at the sun beginning to set above the endless Pacific horizon. "I mean, there isn't even a here *to* stop at. And before long it'll be getting dark…"

"Yeah, well, you tell that to Magwitch's fine hunk of Detroit dogshit here, babycakes," and Tam opens her door, slams it closed behind her and leaves the twins staring at each other in silent, astonished panic.

Lark tries to open her door, then, but it's pressed smack up against the guardrail and there's not enough room to squeeze out, just three or four scant inches and that's not even space for her waif's boneangle shoulders. So she slides her butt across the faded, green naugahyde, accidentally knocks the box of tapes over and they spill in a plastic loud clatter across the seat and into the floorboard. She sits behind the wheel while Crispin climbs over from the back seat. Tam's standing in front of the car now, staring furiously down at the hood, and Crispin whispers, "If you let off the brake, maybe we could run over her," and Lark reaches beneath the dash like maybe it's not such a bad idea, but she only pulls the hood release.

"She'd live, probably," Lark says, and "Yeah," Crispin says, and begins to gather up the scattered cassettes and return them to the dingy shoebox.

The twins sit together on the guardrail while Tam curses the traitorous, steamhissing car, curses her ignorance of wires and rubber belts and radiators, and curses absent Magwitch for owning the crappy old Impala in the first place.

"He said it runs hot sometimes, and to just let it cool off," Crispin says hopefully and she shuts him up with a razorshard glance. So he holds Lark's hand and stares at a bright patch of California poppies growing on the other side of the rail, a tangerineorange puddle of blossoms waving heavy, calyx heads in the salt and evergreen breeze. A few minutes more and Lark and Crispin both grow bored with Tam's too-familiar indignation, tiresome rerun of a hundred other tantrums, and they slip away together into the flowers.

"It's probably not as bad as she's making it out to be," Crispin says, picking a poppy and slipping the sapbleeding stem behind Lark's right ear. "It just needs to cool off."

"Yeah," she says, "Probably," but not sounding reassured at all, and stares down the precarious steep slope toward the beach, sand the cinder color of cold apocalypse below the gray shale and sandstone bluff. She also picks a poppy and puts it in Crispin's hair, tucks it behind his left ear, so they match again. "I want to look for sea shells," she says "and driftwood," and she points at a narrow trail just past the poppies. Crispin looks back at Tam once, her black hair wild in the wind, her face in her hands like maybe she's even crying, and then he follows Lark.

Mostly just mussels, long shells darker than the beach, curved and flaking like diseased toenails, but Lark puts a few in her purse, anyway. Crispin finds a single crab claw, almost as orange as the poppies in their hair with an airbrush hint of blue, and she keeps that too. The driftwood is more plentiful, but all the really good pieces are gigantic, the warped and polished bones of great trees washed down from the mountains and scattered about here, shattered skeletons beyond repair. They walk on warm sand and a thick mat of sequoia bark and spindletwigs, fleshy scraps of kelp, follow the flotsam to a stream running down to meet the gently crashing sea, shallowwide interface of saltwater and fresh. Overhead, seagulls wheel and protest the intrusion; the craggy rocks just offshore are covered with their watchful numbers, powdergray feathers, white feathers, beaks for snatching fish. *And pecking eyes*, Lark thinks. They squawk and stare and she gives them the finger, one nail chewed down to the quick and most of the black polish flaked away.

Crispin bends and lets the stream gurgle about his pale hands. It's filled with polished stones, muted olive and bottle green pebbles rounded by their centuries in the cold water. He puts one finger to his lips and licks it cautiously and "Sweet," he says. "It's very sweet."

"What's that?" Lark says and he looks up, across the stream at a windstunted stand of firs on the other side and there's a sign there, almost as big as a roadside billboard sign and just as gaudy, but no way anyone could see this from the highway. A great sign of planks painted white and lettered crimson, artful, scrolling letters that spell out, "ALIVE AND UNTAMED! MONSTERS AND MYSTERIES OF NEPTUNE'S BOSOM!" and below, in slightly smaller script, "MERMAIDS AND MIRACLES! THE GREAT SEA SERPENT! MANEATERS AND DEVILFISH!"

"Someone likes exclamation points," Lark says, but Crispin's already halfway across the stream, walking on the knobby stones protruding from the water and she follows him, both arms out for balance like a trapeze acrobat. "Wait," she calls to him, and he pauses, reluctant, until she catches up.

The old house trailer sits a little way up the slope from the beach, just far enough that it's safe from the high tides. Lark and Crispin stand side by side, holding hands tight, and stare up at it, lips parted and eyes wide enough to divulge a hint of their mutual surprise. Lark's left boot is wet where she missed a stone and her foot went into the stream, and the water's beginning to seep past leather straps and buckles, through her hose, but she doesn't notice, or it doesn't matter, because this is that unexpected. This old husk of sunbleached aluminum walls, corrugated metal skin draped in mopgray folds of fishing net, so much netting it's hard to see that the trailer underneath might once have been blue. Like something a giant fisherman dragged up from the sea, and finally, realizing what he had, this inedible hunk of rubbish, he left it here for the gulls and the weather to take care of.

"Wow," Lark whispers, and Crispin turns, looks over his shoulder to see if maybe Tam has given up on the car and come looking for them. But there's only the beach, and the waves, and the birds. The air that smells like dead fish and salt wind, and Crispin asks, "You wanna go see?"

"There might be a phone," Larks says, still whispering. "If there's a phone we could call someone to fix the car."

"Yeah," Crispin replies, like they really need an excuse beyond their curiosity. And there are more signs leading up to the trailer, splinternail bread crumbs teasing them to take the next step, and the next, and the next after that: "THE MOUTH THAT SWALLOWED JONAH!" and "ETERNAL LEVIATHAN AND CHARYBDIS REVEALED!" As they get close they can see other things in the sandy rind of yard surrounding the trailer, the rusting hulks of outboard motors and a ship's wheel nailed to a post, broken lobster cages and the ivorywhite jaws of sharks strung up to dry like toothy laundry. There are huge plywood and canvas façades leaned or hammered against the trailer, one on either side of the narrow door and both taller than the roof: garish seascapes with whitefanged sea monsters breaking the surface, acrylic foam and spray, flailing fins like Japanese fans of flesh and wire, eyes like angry, boiling hemorrhages.

A sudden gust off the beach, then, and they both have to stop and cover their eyes against the blowing sand. The wind clatters and whistles around all the things in the yard, tugs at the sideshow canvases. "Maybe we should go back now," Lark says when the wind has gone, and she brushes sand from her clothes and hair. "She'll wonder where we've gone..."

"Yeah," Crispin says, his voice grown thin and distant, distracted, and "Maybe," he says, but they're both still climbing, past the hand-lettered signs and into the ring of junk. Crispin pauses before the shark jaws, yawning cartilage jaws on nylon fishing line and he runs the tip of one finger lightly across rows of gleaming, serrate triangles, only a little more pressure and he could draw blood.

And then the door of the trailer creaks open and the man is standing in the dark space, not what either expected if only because they hadn't known what to expect. A tall man, gangly knees and elbows through threadbare clothes, pants and shirt the same faded khaki; bony wrists from buttoned sleeves too short for his long arms, arthritis swollen knuckles on his wide hands. Lark makes an uneasy sound when she sees him and Crispin jerks his hand away from the shark's jaw, sneakchild caught in the cookie jar startled, and snags a pinkie, soft skin torn by dentine and he leaves a crimson gleaming drop of himself behind.

"You be careful there, boy," the man says with a voice like water sloshing in a rocky place. "That's *Carcharodon carcharias* herself hanging there and her ghost is just as hungry as her belly ever was. You've given her a taste of blood and she'll remember now..."

"Our car broke down," Lark says to the man, looking up at his face for the first time since the door opened. "And we saw the signs..." She points back down the hill without looking away from the man, his cloudy eyes that seem too big for his skull, odd, forwardsloping skull with more of an underbite than she ever thought possible and a wormpink wrinkle where his lower lip should be, nothing at all for the upper. Eyes set too far apart, wide nostrils too far apart and a scraggly bit of gray beard perched on the end of his sharp chin. Lank hair to his shoulders and almost as gray as the scrap of beard.

"Do you want to see inside, then?" he asks, that watery voice, and Lark and Crispin both look back toward the signs, the little stream cutting the beach in half. There's no evidence of Tam anywhere.

"Does it cost money?" Crispin asks, glances tentatively out at the man from underneath the white shock of hair hiding half his face.

"Not if you ain't got any," the man replies and blinks once, vellum lids fast across those bulging eyes.

"It's getting late and our car's broken down," Lark says and the man makes a noise that might be a sigh or might be a cough. "It don't take long," he says and smiles, shows crooked teeth the color of nicotine stains.

"And you've got all the things that those signs say in there?" Crispin asks, one eyebrow cocked, eager, excited doubt, and the man shrugs.

"If it's free, I don't expect you'll be asking for your money back," as if that's an answer, but enough for Crispin and he nods his head and steps toward the door, away from the shark jaws. But Lark grabs his hand, anxious grab that says "Wait," without using any words, and when he looks at her, eyes that say, "This isn't like the dinosaurs, whatever it is, this isn't plaster and plywood," and so he smiles for her, flashes comfort and confidence.

"It'll be something cool," he says. "Better than listening to Tam bitch at us about the car, at least."

So she smiles back at him, small and nervous smile and she squeezes his hand a little harder.

"Come on, if you're coming," the man says. "I'm letting in the flies, standing here with the door wide open."

"Yeah," Crispin says. "We're coming," and the man holds the door for them, steps to one side, and the trailer swallows them like a hungry, metal whale.

Inside, and the air is chilly and smells like fish and stagnant saltwater, mildew, and there's the faintest rotten odor somewhere underneath, dead thing washed up and swelling on the sand. Crispin and Lark pause while the man pulls the door shut behind them, shuts them in, shuts the world out. "Do you live in here?" Lark asks, still squeezing Crispin's hand, and the old man turns around, the tall old man with his billygoat beard and looking down on the twins now as he scratches at the scaly, dry skin on his neck.

"I have myself a cot in the back, and a hot plate," he replies and Lark nods; her eyes are adjusting to the dim light leaking in through the dirty windowpanes and she can see the flakes of dead skin, dislodged and floating slowly down to settle on the dirty linoleum floor of the trailer.

The length of the trailer has been lined with wooden shelves and huge glass tanks and there are sounds to match the smells, wet sounds, the constant bubble of aquarium pumps, water filters, occasional, furtive splashes.

"Wonders from the blackest depths," the old man sighs, wheezes, sicklytired imitation of a carnie barker's spiel, and "Jewels and nightmares plucked from Davy Jones' Locker, washed up on the shores of the Seven Seas..."

The old man is interrupted by a violent fit of coughing and Crispin steps up to the nearest shelf, a collection of jars, dozens and dozens of jars filled with murky ethanol or formalin, formaldehyde weakteabrown and the things that float lifelessly inside: scales and spines, oystergray flesh and lidless, unseeing eyes like pickled grapes. Labels on the jars, identities in a spideryfine handwriting, and the paper so old and yellow he knows that it would crumble at his most careful touch.

The old man clears his throat, loud, phlegmy rattle and he spits into a shadowmoist corner.

"Secrets from the world's museums, from Mr. Charles Darwin's own cabinets, scooped from the sea off Montevideo in eighteen-hundred and thirty-two..."

"Is that an octopus?" Lark asks and the twins both stare into one of the larger jars, three or four gallons and a warty lump inside, a bloom of tentacles squashed against the glass like something wanting out. Crispin presses the tip of one finger to the glass, traces the outline of a single, dimewide suction cup.

The old man coughs again, throaty raw hack, produces a wadded and wrinkled, snotstained handkerchief from his shirt pocket and wipes at his wide mouth with it.

"*That*, boy, is the larva of the Kraken, the greatest of the cephalopods, Viking-bane, ten strangling arms to hale dragon ships beneath the waves." And then the old man clears his throat, and, in a different voice, barker turned poet, recites, "'Below the thunders of the upper deep, / Far, far beneath in the abysmal sea, / His ancient, dreamless, uninvaded sleep / The Kraken sleepeth...'"

"Tennyson," Lark says and the old man nods, pleased.

Crispin leans closer, squints through the gloom and dusty glass, the clouded preserving fluids, and now he can see something dark and sharp like a parrot's beak nested at the center of the rubbery molluskflower. But then they're being hurried along, past all the unexamined jars, and here's the next stop on the old man's tour.

Beneath a bell jar, the taxidermied head and arms and torso of a monkey sewn onto the dried tail of a fish, the stitches plain to see, but he tells them it's a baby mermaid, netted near the coast of Java a hundred years ago.

"It's just half an old, dead monkey with a fish tail stuck on," Crispin says, impertinent, already tiring of these moldy, fabricated wonders. "See?" and he points at the stitches in case Lark hasn't noticed them for herself.

The old man makes an annoyed sound, not quite anger, but impatience, certainly, and he moves them quickly along, this time to a huge fish tank, plateglass sides so overgrown with algae there's no seeing *what's* inside, just mossygreen like siren hair that sways in whatever dull currents the aquarium's pump is making.

"I can't see anything at all in there," Crispin says, as Lark looks nervously back past the mermaid toward the trailer door. But Crispin stands on his toes, peers over the edge of the tank, and "You need to put some snails in there," he says. "To eat some of that shit so people can see..."

"*This* one has no name, no proper name," the old man croaks through his snotclogged throat. "No legend. This one was scraped off the hull of a Russian whaler with the shipworms and barnacles and on Midsummer's Eve, put an ear to the glass and you'll hear it *singing* in the language of riptides and typhoons."

And something seems to move, then, maybe, beyond the emerald scum, feathery red gillflutter or a thousand jointed legs the color of a burn and Crispin jumps, steps away from the glass and lets go of Lark's hand. Smug grin on the old man's long face to show his yellowed teeth, and he makes a barking noise like seals or laughing.

"You go back, if you're getting scared," the old man says and Lark looks like that's all she wants in the world right now, to be out of the trailer, back on the beach and headed up the cliff to the Impala. But Crispin takes her hand again, this very same boy that's afraid of banana slugs but something here he has to see, something he has to prove to himself or to the self-satisfied old man and "What's next, sea monkeys?" he asks, defiant, mock brave.

"Right here," the old man says, pointing to something more like a cage than a tank, "The spawn of the great sea serpent and a Chinese water dragon," planks and chicken wire on the floor, almost as tall as the twins and Crispin drags Lark along toward it. "Tam will be looking for us, won't she?" she asks, but he ignores her, stares instead into the enclosure. There's muddy straw on the bottom and motionless coils of gold and chocolatebrown muscle.

"Jesus, it's just a stupid python, Lark. See? It's not even as big as the one that Alexandra used to have. What a rip-off..." and then he stops, because the snake moves, shifts its chainlink bulk and now he can see its head, the tiny horns above its pearlbead eyes, and further back, a single, stubby flap of meat along one side of its body that beats nervously at the air a moment and then lies still against the filthy straw.

"There's something wrong with it, Crispin, that's all," Lark says, argument to convince herself, and the old man says, "She can crush a full-grown pig in those coils, or a man," and he pauses for the drama, then adds, resuming his confident barker cadence, sly voice to draw midway crowds—"Kept inside a secret Buddhist monastery on the Yangtze and worshipped for a century, and all the sacrificial children she could eat," he says.

The flipper thing on its side moves again, vestigial limb rustle against the straw, and the snake flicks a tongue the color of gangrene and draws its head slowly back into its coils, retreating, hiding from their sight or the dim trailer light or both; "Wonders from the blackest depths," the old man whispers, "Mysteries of the deep, spoils of the abyss," and Lark is all but begging, now. "*Please*, Crispin. We should go," but her voice almost lost in the burbling murmur of aquarium filters.

Crispin's hand about her wrist like a steel police cuff, and she thinks, *How much more can there be, how much can this awful little trailer hold?* When she looks back the way they've come, past the snake-thing's cage and the green tank and the phony mermaid, past all the jars, it seems a long, long way; the dizzying impression that the trailer's somehow bigger inside than out and she shivers, realizes that she's sweating, clammy coldsweat in tiny salt beads on her upper lip, across her forehead and leaking into her eyes. *How much more?* but there's at least *one* more, and they step past a plastic shower curtain, slick blue plastic printed with cartoon sea horses and starfish and turtles, to stand before the final exhibit in the old man's shabby menagerie.

"Dredged from the bottom of Eel Canyon off Humboldt Bay, hauled up five hundred fathoms through water so inky black and cold it might be the very moment before Creation itself," and Crispin is staring at something Lark can't see, squinting into the last tank; cold pools about Lark's ankles, one dry and one still wet from the stream, sudden, tangible chill that gathers itself like the old man's words of cold, or heavy air spilling from an open freezer door.

"And this was just a *scrap*, boy, a shred ripped from the haunches or seaweed-crusted skull of a behemoth..."

"I can't see anything," Crispin says, and then, "*Oh*. Oh shit. Oh, Jesus..."

Lark realizes where the cold is coming from, that it's pouring out from under the shower curtain and she slips her sweatgreased hand free of Crispin's grasp. He doesn't even seem to notice, can't seem to stop staring into the murky, ill-lit tank that towers over them, fills the rear of the trailer from wall to wall.

"And *maybe*," the old man says, bending very close and he's almost whispering to Crispin now, secrets and suspicions for the boy twin and no one else. "Maybe it's growing itself a whole new body in there, a whole new organism from that stolen bit of flesh, like the arm of a starfish that gets torn off..."

Lark touches the folds of the curtain and the cold presses back from the other side. Cold that would burn her hand if she left it there, lingered long enough. She glances back at the old man and Crispin to be sure they're not watching, because she knows this must be forbidden, something she's not meant to see. And then she pulls one corner of the shower curtain aside, and that terrible cold flows out, washes over her like a living wave of arctic breath and a neglected cat box smell and another, sharper odor like cabbage left too long at the bottom of a refrigerator.

"Fuck," Crispin says behind her. "No fucking way," and the old man is reciting Tennyson again.

"There hath he lain for ages, and *will* lie / Battening upon huge sea worms in his sleep, / Until the latter fire shall heat the deep..."

There is dark behind the shower curtain, dark like a wall, solid as the cold, and again, that vertigo sense of a vast space held somehow inside the little trailer, that this blackness might go on for miles. That she could step behind the curtain and spend her life wandering lost in the alwaysnight collected here.

"...Then once by man and angels to be seen," the old man says, somewhere back there in the World, where there is simple light and warmth, "In roaring he shall rise and on the surface die."

Far off, in the dark, there are wet sounds, something breaking the surface of water that has lain so still so long and she can feel its eyes on her then, eyes made to see where light is a fairy tale and the sun a murmured heresy. The sound of something vast and sinuous coming slowly through the water toward her and Crispin says, "It moved, didn't it? Jesus, it fucking *moved* in there."

It's so close now, Lark thinks. *It's so close and this is the worst place in the world and I* should *be scared, I should be scared shitless.*

"Sometimes it moves," the old man says. "In its sleep, sometimes it moves."

Lark steps over the threshold, the thin, tightrope line between the trailer and this place, ducks her head beneath the shower curtain and the smell is stronger than ever now. It gags her and she covers her mouth with one hand, another step and the curtain will close behind her and there will be nothing but this perfect, absolute cold and darkness and her and the thing swimming through the black. Not really water in there, she knows, just *black* to hide it from the prying, jealous light—and then Crispin has her hand again, is pulling her back into the blinding glare of the trailer and the shower curtain falls closed with an unforgiving, disappointed *shoosh*. The old man and his fishlong face is staring at her, his rheumy, accusing eyes, and "That was not for you, girl," he says. "I did not show you that..."

She almost resists, wrenches her hand free of Crispin's and slips back behind the curtain before anyone can stop her, the only possible release from the sudden emptyhollow feeling eating her up inside, like waking from a dream of Heaven or someone dead alive again, the glimpse of anything so pure and then it's yanked away. But Crispin is stronger and the old man is blocking the way, anyhow, grizzled Cerberus standing guard before the aquamarine plastic, a faint string of drool at one corner of his mouth.

"Come on, Lark," Crispin says to her. "We shouldn't be here. We shouldn't ever have come in here."

The look in the old man's eyes says he's right and already the dream is fading, whatever she might have seen or heard already bleeding away in the last, watercolor dregs of daylight getting into the trailer.

"I'm sorry," Crispin says as they pass the shriveled mermaid and he pushes the door open, not so far back after all, "I didn't want you to think I was afraid."

And "No," she says, "No," doesn't know what to say next, but it doesn't really matter, because they're stumbling together down the trailer's concrete block steps, their feet in the sand again, and the air is filled with gentle twilight and the screaming of gulls.

Tam has been standing by the stream for half an hour, at least that long since she wandered down to the beach looking for the twins, after the black man in the pick-up truck stopped and fixed the broken fan belt, used an old pair of pantyhose from the back seat of the Impala and then refilled the radiator. "You take it easy, now, and that oughta hold far as San Francisco," he said, but then she couldn't find Lark or Crispin. Her throat hurts from calling them, near dark now and she's been standing here where their footprints end at the edge of the water, shouting their names. Getting angrier, getting fucking scared, the relief that the car's running again melting away, deserting her for visions of the twins drowned or the twins lost or the twins raped and murdered.

Twice she started across the stream, one foot out and plenty enough stones between her and the other side to cross without getting her feet wet, and twice she stopped. Thought that she glimpsed dark shapes moving just below the surface, undulating forms like the wings of stingrays or the tentacles of an octopus or squid, black and eellong things darting between the rocks. And never mind that the water is crystal clear and couldn't possibly be more than a few inches deep. Never mind she *knows* it's really nothing more than shadow tricks and the last glimmers of the setting sun caught in the rippling water. These apprehensions too instinctual, the thought of what might be waiting for her if she slipped, sharp teeth eager for stray ankles, anxiety all but too deep to question, and so she's stood here, feeling stupid, calling them like she was their goddamn mother.

She looks up again and there they are, almost stumbling down the hill, the steep dirt path leading down from the creepy old trailer, Crispin in the lead and dragging Lark along, a cloud of dust trailing out behind them. When they reach the stream they don't even bother with the stepping stones, just splash their way straight across, splashing her in the bargain.

"Mother*fucker*," Tam says and steps backwards onto drier sand. "Will you please watch what the fuck you're doing? Shit..." But neither of them says a word, stand breathless at the edge of the stream, the low bank carved into the sand by the water; Crispin stares down at his soggy Docs and Lark glances nervously back toward the trailer on the hill.

"Where the hell have you two bozos been? Didn't you hear me calling you? I'm fucking hoarse from calling you."

"An old man," Lark gasps, wheezes the words out, and before she can say anything else Crispin says, "A sideshow, Tam, that's all," speaking quickly like he's afraid of what Lark will say if he doesn't, what she might have been about to say. "Just some crazy old guy with a sort of a sideshow."

"Jesus," Tam sighs, pissytired sigh that she hopes sounds the way she feels and she reaches out and plucks a wilted poppy from Crispin's hair, tosses it to the sand at their feet. "That figures, you know? That just fucking figures. Next time, Magwitch comes or your asses stay home," and she turns her back on them, then, heading up the beach toward the car. She only stops once, turns around to be sure they're following and they are, close behind and their arms tight around one another's shoulders as if they couldn't make it alone. The twins' faces are hidden in shadow, nightshrouded, and behind them, the sea has turned a cold, silvery indigo and stretches away to meet the rising stars.

Born near Dublin, Ireland, Caitlín R. Kiernan has lived most of her life in the southeastern United States. Trained as a vertebrate paleontologist, she spent much of the 1980's working for museums and researching extinct marine reptiles, until she began pursuing fiction writing full time in 1992. Her first story sold to Steve Rasnic Tem's anthology, *High Fantastic,* in July 1993, and since then, her gothic and gothnoir short fiction has appeared in numerous anthologies, including *The Sandman: Book Of Dreams, Love In Vein II, Lethal Kisses, Darkside: Horror For The Next Millennium, Noirotica 2, Brothers Of The Night, Dark Terrors 2* and *3, Secret City: Strange Tales Of London, Dark Of The Night, Years Best Horror-1997,* and *The Year's Best Fantasy And Horror #11.* Her first novel, *Silk,* was released by Penguin (Roc), with limited and deluxe-limited editions available soon from Darkside Press. Caitlín is currently scripting *The Dreaming* for DC Comics and developing other projects for DC's Vertigo line. She lives in a renovated overall factory in Birmingham, Alabama.

Website: Pandora Station - www.gothic.net/pandora

Come check out our web site for details on these Meisha Merlin authors!

Kevin J. Anderson
Storm Constantine
Keith Hartman
Tanya Huff
Janet Kagan
Caitlín R. Kiernan
Lee Killough
Sharon Lee & Steve Miller
Adam Niswander
Selina Rosen
Kristine Kathryn Rusch
S. P. Somtow
Allen Steele

http://www.angelfire.com/biz/MeishaMerlin

Now back in print are Lee Killough's
Blood Hunt and *Bloodlinks*.

Together for the first time in one Volume:
BloodWalk

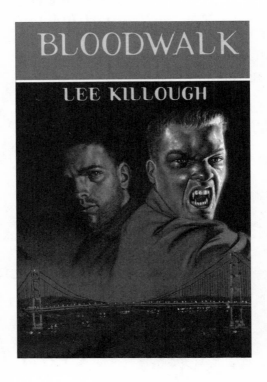

Visit our web site or write us at the address below for
ordering information

Meisha Merlin Publications, Inc
PO Box 7
Decatur, GA 30031